ADVENTURES

Robin
and the Knight

Tales of Robin Hood

First published in 2006 by
Franklin Watts
338 Euston Road
London
NW1 3BH

Franklin Watts Australia
Level 17/207 Kent Street
Sydney
NSW 2000

A CIP catalogue record for this book is available
from the British Library.

ISBN 978 0 7496 6699 6

Series Editor: Jackie Hamley
Series Advisor: Dr Barrie Wade
Series Designer: Peter Scoulding

Printed in China

Franklin Watts is a
Hachette Children's books,
an Hachette Livre t
www.hachettelivre.

HOPSCOTCH ADVENTURES

Robin
and the Knight

by Damian Harvey and Martin Remphry

W
FRANKLIN WATTS
LONDON•SYDNEY

Robin Hood and Little John
were hiding by the road, hoping
a rich knight or a greedy
bishop might pass by.

"I can hear someone," said Robin.
"It looks like a rich, lazy knight,"
said Little John. "Let's take his
money to give to the poor."

But as he rode closer, Robin and Little John could see the knight's clothes were torn and dirty.

"Welcome to Sherwood Forest," said Robin. "Friar Tuck is preparing a feast. I'd be pleased if you'd eat with me and my merry men tonight."

"Thank you," said the knight.

"I am Sir Richard."

"I had hoped for more than your thanks," said Robin.

"I see," said Sir Richard, "but ten silver pennies are all I have."

"Why does a noble knight only have
ten silver pennies?" asked Robin.

"It is a sad tale," said Sir Richard. "My son was in a jousting tournament, and he beat many great knights."

"All was well until the final joust against Sir Walter. Their lances broke and Sir Walter was accidentally killed.

"My son was arrested and thrown into jail. He would have died if I had not paid his ransom."

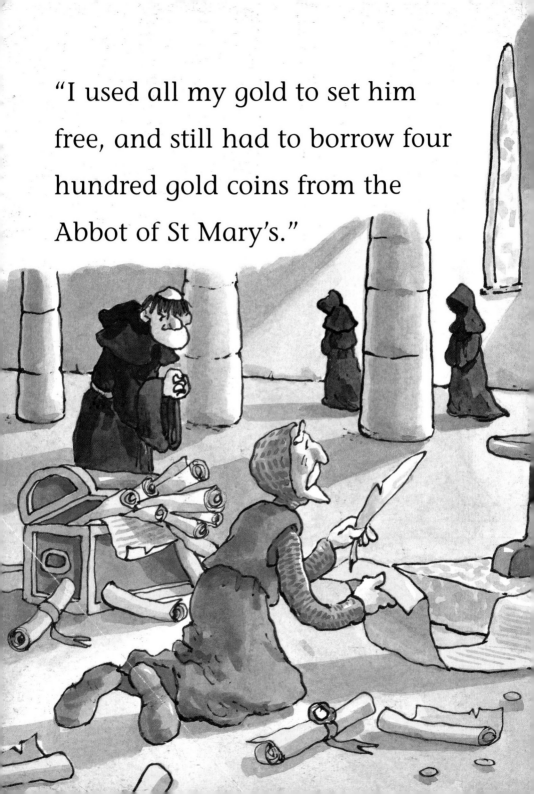

"I used all my gold to set him free, and still had to borrow four hundred gold coins from the Abbot of St Mary's."

"Now, unless I repay the Abbot in three days, my castle and land will belong to him."

"Four hundred gold coins for your castle and land!" cried Robin Hood. "That Abbot is too greedy."

Robin Hood sent Will Scarlet to count out four hundred gold coins from their secret treasure store.

Robin gave the money to Sir Richard.

"Take this as a loan," he said.

"You can pay your debt to the

Abbot and repay me when you can."

Sir Richard went straight
to see the Abbot.

"Here are your four hundred gold coins," said Sir Richard. "Now keep your hands off my home!"

Next day, Robin and Little John
were walking by the road.
"I wish we could teach that greedy
Abbot a lesson," said Robin.

"Perhaps we can," said Little John.

"Here comes one of his monks."

"Welcome!" said Robin.

"Will you join us for a feast?"

"No!" said the monk.

"I have no money."

"If you have no money," said Little John, "these four hundred gold coins must be ours."

"There," said Robin.
"Our pockets are full again,
and Sir Richard doesn't have
to pay back his loan."

"But my stomach is still empty," said Little John.
"Come on," said Robin.
"We have a feast waiting!"

Hopscotch has been specially designed to fit the requirements of the Literacy Framework. It offers real books by top authors and illustrators for children developing their reading skills.

ADVENTURES

Aladdin and the Lamp
ISBN 978 0 7496 6692 7

Blackbeard the Pirate
ISBN 978 0 7496 6690 3

George and the Dragon
ISBN 978 0 7496 6691 0

Jack the Giant-Killer
ISBN 978 0 7496 6693 4

TALES OF KING ARTHUR

1. The Sword in the Stone
ISBN 978 0 7496 6694 1

2. Arthur the King
ISBN 978 0 7496 6695 8

3. The Round Table
ISBN 978 0 7496 6697 2

4. Sir Lancelot and the Ice Castle
ISBN 978 0 7496 6698 9

TALES OF ROBIN HOOD

Robin and the Knight
ISBN 978 0 7496 6699 6

Robin and the Monk
ISBN 978 0 7496 6700 9

Robin and the Silver Arrow
ISBN 978 0 7496 6703 0

Robin and the Friar
ISBN 978 0 7496 6702 3

FAIRY TALES

The Emperor's New Clothes
ISBN 978 0 7496 7421 2

Cinderella
ISBN 978 0 7496 7417 5

Snow White
ISBN 978 0 7496 7418 2

Jack and the Beanstalk
ISBN 978 0 7496 7422 9

The Three Billy Goats Gruff
ISBN 978 0 7496 7420 5

The Pied Piper of Hamelin
ISBN 978 0 7496 7419 9

Goldilocks and the Three Bears
ISBN 978 0 7496 7903 3

Hansel and Gretel
ISBN 978 0 7496 7904 0

The Three Little Pigs
ISBN 978 0 7496 7905 7

Rapunzel
ISBN 978 0 7496 7906 4

Little Red Riding Hood
ISBN 978 0 7496 7907 1

Rumpelstiltskin
ISBN 978 0 7496 7908 8

HISTORIES

Toby and the Great Fire of London
ISBN 978 0 7496 7410 6

Pocahontas the Peacemaker
ISBN 978 0 7496 7411 3

Grandma's Seaside Bloomers
ISBN 978 0 7496 7412 0

Hoorah for Mary Seacole
ISBN 978 0 7496 7413 7

Remember the 5th of November
ISBN 978 0 7496 7414 4

Tutankhamun and the Golden Chariot
ISBN 978 0 7496 7415 1

MYTHS

Icarus, the Boy Who Flew
ISBN 978 0 7496 7992 7 *
ISBN 978 0 7496 8000 8

Perseus and the Snake Monster
ISBN 978 0 7496 7993 4 *
ISBN 978 0 7496 8001 5

Odysseus and the Wooden Horse
ISBN 978 0 7496 7994 1 *
ISBN 978 0 7496 8002 2

Persephone and the Pomegranate Seeds
ISBN 978 0 7496 7995 8 *
ISBN 978 0 7496 8003 9

Romulus and Remus
ISBN 978 0 7496 7996 5 *
ISBN 978 0 7496 8004 6

Thor's Hammer
ISBN 978 0 7496 7997 2*
ISBN 978 0 7496 8005 3

No Dinner for Anansi
ISBN 978 0 7496 7998 9 *
ISBN 978 0 7496 8006 0

Gelert the Brave
ISBN 978 0 7496 7999 6*
ISBN 978 0 7496 8007 7

* hardback